SuperGoldfish

By
Jacqueline H. Faber

Illustrated by
N.D. Engleson

Balboa Press books may be ordered through booksellers or by contacting:

Balboa Press
A Division of Hay House
1663 Liberty Drive
Bloomington, IN 47403
www.balboapress.com
844-682-1282

Because of the dynamic nature of the Internet, any web addresses or links contained in this
book may have changed since publication and may no longer be valid. The views expressed
in this work are solely those of the author and do not necessarily reflect the views of
the publisher, and the publisher hereby disclaims any responsibility for them.

Any people depicted in stock imagery provided by Getty Images are models,
and such images are being used for illustrative purposes only.
Certain stock imagery © Getty Images.

ISBN: 978-1-9822-6358-4 (sc)
ISBN: 978-1-9822-7356-9 (hb)
ISBN: 978-1-9822-6359-1 (e)

Library of Congress Control Number: 2021902821

Print information available on the last page.

Balboa Press rev. date: 02/27/2021

Dedicated to Melinda and Tyler for your inspiration.

"Where there is hatred, let there be love." St. Francis

Fast as a speeding swordfish. Brave as a daring dolphin. Kind as a papa sea horse. It's SuperGoldfish!—protector of guppies and goldfish in the tank they all call home.

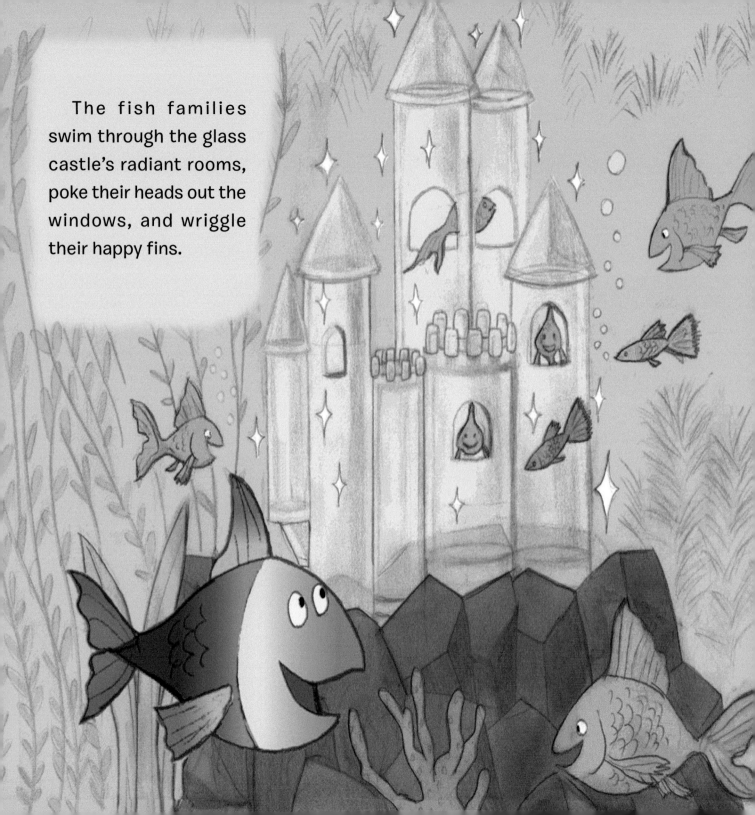

The fish families swim through the glass castle's radiant rooms, poke their heads out the windows, and wriggle their happy fins.

Until one day–SPLASH!

Tiger Barb charges the castle. He snaps his spiky teeth. "Mine! This castle is mine!"

The guppies and goldfish flee.

SuperGoldfish rises up on his tail fin, "We all share the castle!"

"Skedaddle, puny fish!" Tiger Barb lunges at SuperGoldfish. He shoots a stinky bonk-bubble at him.

"Pee-yew!" SuperGoldfish says, "That's disgusting."

"Watch out, SuperGoldfish!" the guppies cry.

Tiger Barb shoots a steam of sticky wonk bubbles. Wonk! Bonk! Thonk!

Bubbles cling to SuperGoldfish.

"Ow-Ow-Ow!

I'll be back, Tiger Barb!"

SuperGoldfish darts into the fern forest. He rubs past Java Fern. Pop! Pop! Pop!
"Java, can I borrow one of your branches?"

She sways in the current. "Here! Take this one."

"Thanks! Now I can bop terrible Tiger Barb!"

SuperGoldfish swims back and looks Tiger Barb in the eye.
Like a dolphin, he rises on his tail fin and puffs out his chest.
"Release our castle!"

"I don't think so, little pipsqueak." Tiger Barb lunges at SuperGoldfish.

With the speed of a swordfish,
SuperGoldfish dodges his spiky teeth.
"Look out!" the goldfish shriek.

Bap! Bap! Bap! Tiger Barb shoots another batch of bonking-bubbles.

SuperGoldfish bats the bubbles back! He raises his branch high to bop the beast. But wait!

Instead, he whirls his branch round and round and round.
Tiger Barb's bubbles boomerang and stick to him like glue.

"Pee-yew!" Tiger Barb cries as his stinky bubbles turn him blue!
His eyes roll up.

He flops over and sinks,
Down . . .
Down . . .
Down to the bottom of the tank.

All the fish circle round, wave their fins and cheer, "Yay, SuperGoldfish! You defeated Tiger Barb without a fin-fight, a bite, or a bop! Way to go!"

The gleeful fish return home to the castle and decorate its walls with angel shells, cowries, and kelp. They swim through its radiant rooms, poke their heads out the windows, and wriggle their happy fins.

But SuperGoldfish wonders:
Where's Tiger Barb?
He dives deep to find him.
"There you are. Are you all right?"
"Why do you care?"
"Were all in this tank together."

Tiger Barb burps a bonking bubble. "What can I do?"
"Be kind."

"But how? I'm a meanie... and a natural nipper."
"Stop bonking and biting. Share the castle."
"Really? I can do that."

They swim. Up Up Up-to the castle.

Tiger Barb glows. SuperGoldfish is his first ever friend.

The fish families giggle full-gill, dance and zip around.
The guppies clap their fins and the goldfish cheer.

SuperGoldfish folds a fond fin around Tiger Barb, his newfound friend.

Fish Facts For Aquariums and Oceans

Goldfish, guppies, and tiger barbs might be able to survive in the same tank, but they would not be happy. Each needs a different temperature. Goldfish like cool water between 68 and 74 degrees, about the same temperature as our homes.

Guppies are tropical fish and like it warmer, between 72 and 78 degrees. Their offspring are called "fry," and are born tiny, but fully formed and self-sufficient.

Tiger Barbs like it warmer still, between 77-82 degrees. They are such naturally aggressive fish they aren't put in tanks with goldfish and guppies.

Goldfish and guppies can live in the same tank, but guppies nip at small goldfishes' fins. Then, when the goldfish get big enough, they can eat their tormentors.

Some of the other creatures would not be found in a home aquarium. Dolphins are way too big and live in saltwater oceans. They aren't fish; they're mammals. Thirty-six species inhabit warm waters around the world. Most are grey, some are pink, and one is black-and-white! Sadly, some species are endangered.

Swordfish are also big and live in oceans. They have long, flat, pointed bills like swords, with nubs along the edges. Adult swordfish are not armed to the teeth because they have no teeth at all! They are very fast, reaching top speeds of 22 miles per hour.

Papa seahorses are tiny, and they too live in the ocean. Their elaborate mating dance is swimming in pairs with their tails linked together, bobbing up and down in the sea grass. In all 50 species the females transfer their eggs to a pouch in the males, where they grow into tiny babies. Each male can give birth to as many as 2000 miniature seahorses at one time.